RUN!

The elephant weighs a ton!

Also by Adam Frost

Stop! There's a Snake in Your Suitcase!

More animal adventures with the
Nightingale family coming soon!

RUN!

The elephant
weighs a ton!

Adam Frost

Illustrated by
Mark Chambers

LONDON NEW DELHI NEW YORK SYDNEY

*All of the animal facts in this story are true.
Everything else is fiction. Any connection
to any events that have taken place in London
Zoo is purely coincidental.*

Bloomsbury Publishing, London, New Delhi, New York and Sydney

First published in Great Britain in September 2012 by Bloomsbury Publishing Plc
50 Bedford Square, London, WC1B 3DP

Manufactured and supplied under licence from the Zoological Society of London

Text copyright © Adam Frost 2012
Illustrations copyright © Mark Chambers 2012

The moral rights of the author and illustrator have been asserted

A CIP catalogue record for this book is available from the British Library

ISBN 978 1 4088 2707 9

MIX
Paper from
responsible sources
FSC® C020471
FSC
www.fsc.org

Typeset by Hewer Text UK Ltd, Edinburgh
Printed and Bound by CPI Group (UK) Ltd, Croydon CR0 4YY

1 3 5 7 9 10 8 6 4 2

www.storiesfromthezoo.com
www.bloomsbury.com
www.adam-frost.com

To Samuel Babich

Chapter 1

'Can't believe we got roped into this,' Tom Nightingale whispered to his best friend, Freddy Finch.

It was the night of the school concert and Tom and Freddy were standing in the wings, waiting to go onstage. Tom was holding his trumpet and Freddy was holding his oboe. The hall was packed with parents and teachers and family friends. Mr McCluskey, the Head Teacher, was standing in front of the curtains, thanking everyone for coming on such a cold evening.

Tom was starting to feel a bit jittery. His hair, which normally stuck up at the back, had been plastered down on to his head and he was wearing a bright white shirt and a dark blue tie. Freddy's hair was in a side parting and he was wearing a black blazer that was far too big for him.

'Are you nervous?' Tom asked Freddy.

'Er, no, course not,' replied Freddy, looking terrified. 'How about you?'

'Oh, er, no way,' said Tom, trying to remember whether he'd already been to the toilet or ought to go again.

'And here they are, the Junior School Orchestra!' declared Mr McCluskey.

There was no more time to feel nervous. The curtain had risen and Mrs Purcell, the music teacher, was leading them out on to the stage.

Tom had to concentrate. They were going to be playing 'When the Saints Go Marching In' and Tom had only ever played it through twice without making a mistake.

Freddy had already admitted that he was going to pretend to play his oboe. He said to Tom that

Olivia Darnell made such a racket on her violin that you couldn't hear anyone else anyway.

But Tom loved his trumpet. He wanted to play it well. Besides, his mum and dad, his grandad and his sister were in the audience. He wanted to put on a good show for them.

Mrs Purcell sat down at a piano on one side of the stage. She craned her neck round and counted them in. Tom took a deep breath and started to play.

He got through the first two bars without any mistakes. He got through the next two bars without any mistakes. He started to relax.

He looked at Freddy pretending to blow down his oboe, but looked away quickly. He didn't want to start laughing into his trumpet.

He kept playing, growing more confident as they reached the second verse. He even felt brave enough to look into the audience and pick out his family in the fifth row.

Everything was going well. He was sailing into the final few bars when he felt his finger

 slip off one of the valves. He missed a note, but recovered quickly and played the next. He played the last few notes slightly out of time, trying to catch up with the rest of the orchestra.

He could feel himself going red. When the audience burst into applause, he couldn't hear it. He was too busy staring straight ahead, looking at nothing, holding his trumpet loosely by his side.

'Five minutes of miming and nobody suspected a thing!' Freddy said to Tom, as they walked offstage.

'Frederick Finch, I'd like a word with you,' said Mrs Purcell, appearing behind them. 'Well done, Tom! YOU were excellent!'

But Tom didn't hear Freddy or Mrs Purcell; he just walked silently backstage.

When the concert was over, he went out into

the hall to meet his family. The hall was still half full, with people smiling and chatting while they waited for their children.

Mrs Nightingale gave her son a big hug. 'I'm so proud of you.'

Mr Nightingale ruffled Tom's plastered-down hair. 'You were brilliant, son.'

Then Grandad hobbled forward, holding his walking stick. 'You're a natural, Tom. A natural!'

Tom looked surprised. 'You mean you didn't hear me mess it up at the end?'

'What are you talking about?' said Sophie. 'You were note perfect.'

'But I got the end totally wrong!' Tom wailed.

'Did you?' The Nightingales looked at each other in surprise and then looked back at Tom.

'Well, if you did, nobody heard it,' Sophie said. 'Honestly.'

At that moment, Mrs Nightingale's phone started to buzz. She glanced down at it.

'It's the zoo,' she said. 'I'm going to answer it and then we're all going out for pizza.'

Mrs Nightingale was Chief Vet at London Zoo, so she had to leave her phone on most of the time. Mr Nightingale worked at the zoo too, as a zookeeper in the large-mammals section. Grandad was retired now, but he had once been Chief Vet just like his daughter.

'Look, Tom,' Mr Nightingale said, crouching down, 'I know you're a perfectionist, but seriously, it sounded amazing.'

Tom shook his head. 'I knew I'd mess it up and I did,' he mumbled.

Mrs Nightingale returned to join them. 'Do you want the good news or the bad news?' she asked.

'Bad,' said Mr Nightingale.

'The vet up at Whipsnade Zoo has caught chickenpox. And they're an elephant keeper down,' said Mrs Nightingale.

'So what's the good news, Mum?' Sophie asked.

'They want me and your dad to spend the summer at Whipsnade.'

'Brilliant!' said Mr Nightingale, giving his wife a big hug.

'It is, isn't it?' said Mrs Nightingale. 'Elephants were my first love as a vet. But I don't really get the chance to work with them that much. They were all moved from London Zoo to Whipsnade years ago to give them more space. Obviously I help up in Whipsnade now and then, but it's not the same as spending the whole summer there.'

'So are we all going?' Sophie asked. 'Where will we stay?'

'Stay?' echoed her mother. 'We'll stay at home, of course.'

'But Whipsnade is miles away,' protested Sophie.

'So we'll move our home a little closer,' said Mrs Nightingale.

The Nightingale family lived on a houseboat just behind the zoo, on Regent's Canal. Grandad had his own boat at the other end of the marina.

Sophie frowned and then a smile spread across her face. 'Ohhh, NOW I get it,' she said.

'We'll sail up the Grand Union Canal!' declared Mrs Nightingale. 'It'll be the school holidays so we can take our time. We'll moor at Apsley and we can all spend every day at Whipsnade.'

'Splendid!' exclaimed Grandad. 'Any excuse for an expedition.'

Tom was beginning to feel excited, but tried not to show it.

Mrs Nightingale turned to him. 'Of course,

if you'd rather stay here and feel sorry for yourself, then that's fine too.'

Tom was silent for a few moments, then he grunted, 'It's OK. I'm fine.'

Sophie took his trumpet. 'Just don't think about this for a few weeks,' she said. 'Leave the trumpeting to the elephants!'

Chapter 2

Two days later, the Nightingale family were on their way to Whipsnade. Mr and Mrs Nightingale's barge led the way, with Grandad's following close behind.

As the boats slid through the water, passers-by turned to watch. It wasn't surprising, seeing as they were two of the most unusual-looking boats on the whole canal.

The Nightingales' barge was nicknamed *The Ark* and was covered from top to bottom in paintings of animals and plants. Every few months, Mr Nightingale would repaint one section, adding new animals. The portholes

were always worked into the design and were currently an egg laid by an ostrich, a bulge in the middle of a boa constrictor and a ball on the end of a seal's nose.

On top of the boat, lots of vegetables grew in flowerpots, and solar panels provided the family with electricity.

Grandad's boat, the *Molly Magee*, was more old-fashioned. Dark green, with a bright red roof, it was covered in hanging baskets and brass ornaments. There was nothing on its roof except for a slightly bent TV aerial.

As they left the marina behind, Tom's memory of the school concert started to fade. He let out a deep sigh. Maybe it hadn't been so bad after all. At one point he even opened his trumpet case and thought about playing one of his favourite pieces. But then he shook his head, snapped the catches back down and slid the case away under his bed.

Instead he spent the days playing with his sister and the family pets. The Nightingales had a terrier called Rex and two cats called Max and Mindy. Tom himself had five stick insects called Hilda, Sven, Rocky, Zeus and Dolores. He'd lost track of his sister's pets: there were definitely ferrets, rats, budgies and goldfish. At one point she'd had a couple of wounded frogs in a tank in her bedroom, but she'd nursed them back to health and released them back into the wild. His sister wanted to be a vet like their mum, so she was always doing things like that.

By the afternoon of the first day, they had reached Perivale. Tom was standing on the rear deck, next to Sophie, who was steering the boat by gently moving a rudder left and right. Rex was leaning over the edge, peering into the water and barking at swans.

Grandad's boat slid along beside them. Soon he was level with them, one hand on the rudder, the other holding a large mug of tea. 'Looking forward to seeing some elephants?' he said.

'Definitely,' said Sophie.

'When I was a young man, I spent a month watching elephants in central Africa,' Grandad began, looking away into the distance.

Tom and Sophie looked at their grandad and grinned. They loved hearing about his weird adventures.

'I remember one day I saw a poacher creeping up on a herd. Now, poachers are the lowest of the low. They kill elephants just to get their ivory tusks. I wanted to stop him, but he had a gun and a big one at that.'

Grandad held his hands apart to show how big the gun was.

'I had to just stand there, watching this brute as he positioned himself behind a rock and took aim. But just as he was about to fire, what do you think happened? A young bull elephant sneaked up behind him and trumpeted right in his ear! The poacher dropped his gun, it went off and a bullet whipped right through his own foot, rather than in the elephant's side! Ha ha ha! Well done, Jumbo!'

14

Tom and Sophie's eyes were wide with amazement.

'See, that's the thing about elephants,' said Grandad. 'Everyone thinks that because they weigh five or six tons, you can hear them coming a mile off. But they have these amazing padded feet. They can move almost silently if they want to. Now, what do we have here?'

Grandad was pointing at a pair of wooden gates in the middle of the canal. There was another pair of wooden gates behind them, and then another and another.

'It's a staircase lock,' he said, 'my favourite kind. Who's going to help me?'

'Me!' Tom and Sophie exclaimed at the same time.

'You both can,' said Grandad.

There were lots of locks on the Grand Union Canal. They were built wherever the water was at two different levels and they allowed barges to move uphill and downhill.

Normally, going through a lock was quite

simple. You opened the gates, moved into the chamber, closed the gates, opened the paddles, the water rushed in, the barge started to rise. When you were the same level as the water on the other side of the lock, you closed the paddles, opened the other gates, and off you went.

But sometimes one lock wasn't enough. The hill was so steep that it took a series of locks to get your boat far enough up or down. The locks were called 'staircase locks' because they ended up looking like a flight of stairs. You had to open

each set of gates and paddles at the right time and in the right order or you could cause a flood.

Tom and Sophie weren't phased though. Tom helped first, turning the windlass in one paddle after another so that all the water in all of the gates was at the right level.

Then they were ready to climb the staircase.

The locks were wide enough to hold two barges, so *The Ark* and the *Molly Magee* went up together.

Sophie and her mother were in charge of the gates, opening them one at a time. Tom and Mr Nightingale stood on the deck of *The Ark*, holding one end of a thick rope. The other end of the rope was thrown around a pillar on the bank and helped to steady the boats when the water rushed into the lock. Grandad was doing the same on the deck of his barge. The boats were jostled back and forth, left and right, occasionally bumping into each other.

Tom held on tightly to the rope, never letting go – no matter how much *The Ark* rocked.

When at last they were at the top of the staircase, the boats sailed out of the final chamber, side by side. Sophie closed the final set of gates and she and her mother hopped back on to *The Ark*.

'Well done, everyone!' Mr Nightingale exclaimed. 'Next stop, the fish and chip shop!'

Chapter 3

Two days later and they were there! They moored at Apsley and went to pick up the van that they had hired for the summer. Then Mr Nightingale, Mrs Nightingale, Tom and Sophie drove to Whipsnade Zoo. Grandad stayed behind at Apsley to sort out the mooring fees.

When the Nightingales got to Whipsnade, Mr Nightingale reported for duty at the elephant house and Mrs Nightingale headed for the hospital. Tom and Sophie were free to do whatever they liked.

They had only been to Whipsnade twice

before, so everything felt new and different and exciting.

Sophie wanted to see the white rhinos and the lions and the giraffes. They were all in the same area, so they headed to these enclosures first. They ran past the Discovery Centre and across the main lawn.

Tom wanted to see the cheetahs. They were just behind the lions, so that was the next stop. They went the long way, through the children's playground and over the Jumbo Express bridge.

They both agreed on what to see after that.

'Elephants,' said Sophie, 'my favourite animal in the world!'

'What happened to snakes?' said Tom, remembering their last adventure and their holiday in Antigua where they had introduced one of the world's rarest snakes back into the wild.

'Snakes are my joint favourite,' Sophie said.

They set off at a jog down towards the elephants' field.

'I hope Dad's there,' Sophie said. 'He might let us feed one of the elephants.'

'Or maybe one of them will squirt water at us!' exclaimed Tom.

'Or perhaps one of them will push a tree over with its head!' Sophie suggested.

They reached the elephants' field and saw a keeper unloading bales of hay from a trailer. They waved at her.

'We're Ed Nightingale's children, Tom and Sophie. We've come to see our dad,' Sophie called out.

The keeper let them into the staff area. Her name was Jane.

Both Tom and Sophie stared at the nine huge animals padding calmly around their large field. Only a fence separated the children from the elephants.

'Your dad's in with Hina,' Jane explained. 'He's giving her a manicure.'

'He's filing an elephant's nails?' Sophie asked.

'Yep,' said Jane. 'Go and have a look if you like.' She nodded at the large grey barn where the elephants slept.

Tom and Sophie ran across to the barn and ducked inside. Their dad was holding a huge file and rasping an elephant's toenail. It couldn't have hurt as the animal was standing patiently with its foot in the air.

Mr Nightingale stopped filing and tapped the elephant's front right foot, saying, 'Hina, lift!'

The elephant obediently put her left foot down and lifted her right foot.

'Are you going to put nail varnish on it too?' Sophie joked.

Mr Nightingale turned round and said, 'Oh he-he-hello, you two.' He was out of breath from all the filing. 'A–As y–you can see, being an elephant keeper can be quite hard work!'

'But what are you doing to her feet, Dad?' Tom asked.

'Well, in the wild, elephants walk for miles and miles each day, looking for food and water. This really wears their nails down. Here, of course, it's different. Yes, we take them out for walks, but basically they spend most of their day in their enclosure. So if we didn't file their nails down, they'd be like daggers. Or spears. OK, Hina, down you go.'

The elephant put her foot down gently.

'So is Hina an African or an Asian elephant? asked Tom.

'Asian, silly,' Sophie said with a sigh. 'Dad's told us this before. For a start, look at her trunk.'

'OK, OK, I remember now,' said Tom. 'An African elephant has . . . er . . . two "fingers" on the end of its trunk.'

'Exactly,' said Sophie, 'and look, Hina's only got one on the end of hers. Then there are her ears. An African elephant has big ears and an Asian elephant like Hina has smaller ears.'

'And African elephants' ears look like a map of Africa, don't they?' Tom said. 'Asian elephants' ears look more like a map of India.'

'You got it,' Mr Nightingale said, leading Hina back into the enclosure.

'I wish human beings were like that too,' said Tom. 'You know, you could tell where they came from just by looking at their ears.'

Sophie smiled and felt one of her ears with her hand.

'So our ears would look like a map of England,' Tom said, 'and Uncle Alphonse's ears would be in the shape of France.'

Once Hina was back in the enclosure, Mr Nightingale, Tom and Sophie came out of the barn and walked across to where Jane was standing.

'Your mum's due here any minute,' she said.

'How come?' Sophie asked. 'Is one of the elephants sick?'

'Not sick,' said Jane, 'but worth keeping an eye on. You can probably guess why.'

Tom and Sophie took a closer look at the nine elephants in the field. There was the large bull, Rudolph: he was in a section all to himself, with a strong locked gate between him and the others. Then there were Hina and six other adult females: Laila, Jeanie, Taz, Betsy, Frieda and Mist. Finally, there was a six-year-old bull called Ricky, who was digging some bark off a log with his tusks.

'Is Mum coming to see that one?' Tom asked, pointing at Rudolph. 'Is he on his own because he's not well?'

'No,' said Jane, 'he's all right. He's on his own because that's how it would be in the wild. Adult males are solitary. They don't like to mix. If you ever see a herd of elephants, it will just be women: sisters, mothers, daughters, nieces. And the odd young bull like Ricky there.'

'Is it that elephant there then?' asked Sophie,

pointing to the female called Laila. She was at the back of the enclosure, not moving much, not doing much.

'Blimey, she's absolutely huge,' said Tom. 'Is Mum going to put her on a diet?'

'She's pregnant, isn't she?' Sophie said to Jane.

'Due any moment,' Jane answered with a smile.

Sophie squeaked with excitement and grabbed Tom's shoulders. 'We're going to see a baby elephant! We're going to see a baby elephant!'

When Sophie had calmed down, Mr Nightingale said to Jane, 'You think it's going to be this week?'

'Definitely,' said Jane. 'We've been recording Laila, and she's growling almost constantly. We think she's telling the rest of the herd that the baby is coming.'

'What do you mean "growling"?' Tom asked. 'I can't hear anything.'

Jane pulled a pair of small headphones out of her pocket and handed them to Tom. When Tom had put them in his ears, Jane pressed Play.

Tom's eyes widened. 'Wow!' he said. He passed the head-phones to Sophie.

'Are you using special equip-ment?' Tom asked.

'No, just a normal MP3 recorder,' Jane said, 'but we're playing it back ten times faster. Elephants speak in such deep voices that we can only hear it if we increase the frequency.'

'It's beautiful,' said Sophie, listening to the slow grumbling noises.

'Elephants talk all the time,' Jane explained. 'They talk when they're happy, when they're sad, when they've found something, when they're ready to move off. We've not been able to listen in till now.'

'So those growls mean, "I'm about to pop"?' Tom asked.

'Something like that.' Jane laughed and nodded. 'The whole herd will help bring up this baby. So Laila needs to let them know it's on its way.'

'Can we use the MP3 player to growl back?' Tom asked. 'Let her know that everything's going to be fine?'

Jane smiled. 'She knows, don't worry. We've been treating her like a princess for the last two years.'

'Two years?!' Tom exclaimed.

'Yep.' Jane nodded. 'Laila has been pregnant for nearly two years. It takes that long to grow an elephant – longer than anything else on Earth. When the calf comes out, it will weigh about one hundred kilos – that's heavier than you two put together.'

Tom and Sophie looked at Laila in wonder. She was padding around majestically in the morning sunshine now, her heavy sides swinging and swaying gently.

'Isn't that the coolest thing you've ever seen?'
Mr Nightingale asked.

Tom and Sophie nodded.

'Me too,' he said.

Chapter 4

Later that evening, when they were back on the barge, Tom and Sophie were still talking about elephants. They both sat on the sofa. Sophie started to leaf through her *Big Book of Massive Mammals* while Tom opened the family laptop and watched a film about baby elephants.

'It says here that elephants have to be born naturally,' said Sophie. 'You can't perform a Caesarean.'

'I think I'm a Caesarean,' said Tom, 'or maybe a Capricorn.'

'Don't be daft, Tom!' exclaimed Sophie. 'Caesarean isn't a star sign. It means the baby has to be cut out of the mother in an operation!'

'Oh, right, yeah, of course,' said Tom. 'But why would you ever do that?'

'If the baby gets stuck or is in distress,' said Sophie, 'or the mother gets sick.'

'OK,' said Tom, 'but why can't an elephant have a Caesarean?'

'They can't have any operations,' said Sophie, glancing down at her book. 'Their skin is so tough and wrinkly that it doesn't heal properly when it's cut. Stitches don't work. Even if you make them out of metal wire.' She looked out of the window. 'I hope Laila's baby will be OK.'

'Course it will,' said Tom. 'Look at all these videos of baby elephants. They get born all the time without any problems.'

Sophie turned to look at the clips on Tom's laptop. 'Let's watch that one,' she said, pointing at a thumbnail of a pregnant African elephant in the Kruger National Park in South Africa.

'I've watched it three times already, but OK,' said Tom.

So Tom and Sophie watched videos of baby elephants for the next half-hour. There was a great one from an American zoo where all the keepers thought that the elephant calf was dead, but the vet said it wasn't and she was right and they built its strength up with heat lamps and lots of water and cow's colostrum. Colostrum is a really thick nutritious kind of milk that female animals produce when their babies are first born.

Another video showed a baby elephant who thought a keeper was its mum. This was because the keeper had hand-reared the calf as the mother elephant was sick.

Mr and Mrs Nightingale came in five minutes later. They had been on Grandad's barge on the other side of the marina, getting some elephant tips. Grandad had helped to deliver several calves when he had been Chief Vet at London Zoo ten years before.

'It's late,' said Mrs Nightingale. 'Time to do your teeth and go to bed.'

'Ohhh,' Tom moaned, 'elephants only need four hours a sleep a night. Why can't we do the same?'

'Brown bats sleep for twenty hours a day,' said Mr Nightingale, 'so it could be worse, don't you think?'

Tom groaned and slunk off to the bathroom.

It was the middle of the night when Mrs Nightingale's mobile phone started to ring. She picked it up, whispered into it for a few seconds and then started to get dressed.

The walls on the barge were very thin, so both Tom and Sophie had been woken up by the noise.

Sophie sat up in her bed and called out through the wall. 'Is it Laila, Mum? Is she having her baby?'

'Go back to sleep,' said Mr Nightingale. 'We're going to get Grandad to come and sit with you.'

Tom got out of bed and stood in the hall.

'Can't we come with you?' he asked. 'We know loads about elephants.'

Mr Nightingale ran his hand through his rumpled hair. Mrs Nightingale pulled on her boots. Mr Nightingale looked at his wife, who shrugged her shoulders.

'OK,' he said. 'Get dressed then. Quickly.'

Forty minutes later, they arrived at the zoo. They ran to the elephant house, where Jane greeted them.

'She's doing really well,' said Jane. 'Maybe twenty minutes to go.'

Mrs Nightingale nodded and followed Jane into the barn. Mr Nightingale led the children into an office where two other keepers and a junior vet called George were already sitting. They'd be able to see everything from there on a video link. Tom and Sophie watched their mother and Jane appear on the screen and inspect Laila from the other side of the barn. Then they disappeared off the screen and came into the office.

'Aren't you staying in there with her?' Sophie asked.

'No, no,' said Mrs Nightingale. 'We don't interfere. She's doing fine by herself. We only get involved if there's a problem.'

So together they watched Laila pushing and pushing. She was bending her back legs and whisking her tail back and forth. For a few minutes, all they could see was the edge of the grey amniotic sac, dangling and bulging between Laila's back legs. Then, suddenly, the calf tumbled out all at once, hitting the ground with a gentle slap, followed by gallons of fluid that soaked the calf from head to toe and rippled across the floor of the barn.

Mr Nightingale and the other elephant keepers cheered. Tom and Sophie joined in.

But Mrs Nightingale was staring at the video screen. She was watching Laila and her calf intently. Laila nudged the calf with her foot and then tried to raise it up with her trunk. The calf just slumped back on its side.

'George, come with me,' Mrs Nightingale said. 'Bring heat lamps. Fluid too. Something's wrong.'

The office was suddenly silent as Mrs Nightingale ducked out of the door.

Tom and Sophie watched the screen in disbelief. Their mother was right. Laila was nudging her baby harder now, almost kicking it. But the little calf just lay there, limp and lifeless.

Tom and Sophie and their dad and the other keepers watched as Mrs Nightingale and George worked. There were heat lamps all around the calf, shining bright, warm light on its shivering body.

Mrs Nightingale was leaning over the baby now, monitoring its heartbeat. 'His pulse is too low,' she said. 'His blood pressure needs to be higher too. And he's having trouble breathing.'

Laila was stamping and fidgeting, clearly distressed.

'It's OK, girl,' Mrs Nightingale whispered, patting her gently. 'It'll be fine.'

'I've got the blood set up,' said George, pointing at a red bag on a metal stand.

'OK, go,' said Mrs Nightingale. George fed a needle into the baby's leg and taped a tube to its skin. Fresh blood started to pump through the calf's body.

A few minutes passed. Mrs Nightingale stared at the monitor. 'It's not working,' she said.

In the office, Sophie murmured, 'It needs milk.'

'What did you say?' Tom asked.

'Do you remember that video?' Sophie said. 'That elephant in the American zoo? They fed it cow's colostrum. To make it stronger. Remember?'

Tom and Sophie told their dad about the video.

'That's true,' he said. 'We did that with a rhino last year. It was the same situation: the baby was too weak to take the mother's milk, and the mother was too distressed to give any of her milk to us. Jane, do you keep cow colostrum on site?'

Jane shook her head. 'I can get some couriered over from the local veterinary college,' she said. 'But it'll take half an hour or so.'

'Well, it's got to be worth a try,' said Mr Nightingale.

Half an hour passed. Mrs Nightingale and George had given the calf more blood and lots of water, which seemed to be helping it breathe more normally and kept its heartbeat steady. But its blood pressure was still low and it didn't want to move. Its trunk curled up once or twice and then thumped back on the straw.

Mrs Nightingale turned to George. 'We need to get some food into him. Do you keep colostrum here?'

'I'll find out,' said George.

As he stood up, Jane came into the barn with some cow's colostrum in a baby's bottle.

'You read my mind,' said Mrs Nightingale.

'Thank your daughter,' said Jane. 'It was her idea.'

'Well done, Sophie,' Mrs Nightingale said to herself. 'You might have just saved this calf's life.'

Jane went back to join the others in the office.

Mrs Nightingale held the bottle over the baby's mouth and let some of the thick liquid drip on to its tongue. The baby didn't react, so she tried again.

The calf's blood pressure was dropping and its heartbeat was starting to slow.

'Come on, you,' encouraged Mrs Nightingale.

Laila was stamping and shuffling again. In the office, Mr Nightingale put his hand over his eyes. 'We're losing him,' he said.

'He's too weak to drink,' said Jane.

The calf gave a deep sigh.

'No, he isn't,' said Sophie. 'Look.'

Mr Nightingale looked back at the screen. The calf had the bottle in its mouth.

'Heartbeat's steady,' said George.

The calf opened its eyes and looked at Mrs Nightingale. It latched on to the bottle again and started to drink.

In the office, Tom turned to his sister. 'Sophie, remember that other video. When the calf was bottle-fed by a keeper, it ended up thinking the keeper was its mum. We've got to stop Mum before the calf gets confused.'

'What was that?' asked Jane.

Tom told Jane what they'd seen.

'You're right,' said Jane. 'I'll go through and tell your mum now.'

Jane went back through into the barn. 'We need to get it to take milk from Laila. So it imprints on her,' she said.

'Yes, I agree,' said Mrs Nightingale, looking down at the calf as it sucked hard on the bottle. She gently removed the bottle from its mouth

42

and squirted some colostrum on to Laila's belly.

The calf started to swirl its trunk around, sniffing the air.

'Milk's over there,' said Mrs Nightingale.

The calf looked everywhere but at its mother.

'Mum's over there,' said Mrs Nightingale.

The calf got to its feet slowly but then fell over. Laila turned around and picked up the calf with her trunk again. This time, the baby stayed on his feet.

His trunk whirled around as he tried to control it. As he walked towards his mother, he nearly tripped over it. He looked over his shoulder at Mrs Nightingale.

'Keep going,' she whispered.

The calf sniffed the air and slapped his mother's side with his trunk.

Laila shuffled her bottom towards him.

The calf took one last look at Mrs Nightingale, then threw his trunk over his head and drank from his mother.

He kept standing and drinking for five minutes, the frizzy hair on his head and back twinkling in the light from the heat lamps.

Mrs Nightingale put her hand on George's shoulder. 'Good work,' she said.

George nodded and smiled. 'You too, boss.'

He started to pack the equipment away.

In the office, everyone was cheering.

'You two were brilliant,' Jane said to Tom and Sophie. 'As a reward, you should get to name him.'

'No? Really?' Sophie said.

'Really,' Jane said.

'Well, there's a boy in my class called Shaurya,' said Tom. 'Apparently it means "Brave Hero" in Hindi.'

'Happy with that, Sophie?' Jane asked.

Sophie thought about it for a second or two. Then she nodded. 'It's perfect.'

Jane smiled. 'Welcome to Whipsnade Zoo, Shaurya!'

Chapter 5

After Shaurya's arrival, the Nightingale family went back to their barge and slept till ten the next morning. Geese honked outside the windows but nobody heard them. Other barges steamed past, gently rocking the boat, but this just sent them into even deeper sleep.

Tom was the first to wake up. He immediately went into his sister's room and stuck his face up to hers.

'Come on, Soph. Let's go and see Shaurya,' he said.

Normally Sophie would have said, 'Go away, Tom,' but this morning she sat bolt upright.

'Ten o'clock! Why didn't you wake me up earlier?'

They went into their parents' room. Mr and Mrs Nightingale had the day off, but they wanted to see Shaurya as much as Tom and Sophie did.

'How long will Shaurya be a child?' Tom asked as they were getting ready to leave. 'Is it a couple of years, like Rex?'

He nodded at the terrier, who was chomping on a dog biscuit in the corner of the kitchen.

'No, elephants are like us,' Mr Nightingale said. 'They're children for a long time. They reach adulthood at about eighteen.'

'Cool, so we'll be able to play with him for years!' Tom exclaimed.

By eleven o'clock, the whole family was watching Shaurya and Laila as they were led from the paddock into the field to meet the other elephants.

'Look what he's doing with his trunk,' Sophie said.

Shaurya had his trunk in his mouth and was sucking it, like a child sucking its thumb.

'Yes, they do that,' said Mrs Nightingale. 'They don't really know what to do with their trunk for the first few months. They put it in their mouth, whirl it around, drag it on the ground . . .'

The other seven elephants were crowding around Shaurya, sniffing him and stroking him with their trunks.

Shaurya was almost invisible behind their

bodies and legs and the dust they were kicking up.

'Is he OK in there?' Tom asked.

'He's more than OK,' Mr Nightingale said. 'Shaurya's family are introducing themselves. All his aunts and sisters. And his big brother, Ricky. They'll all help to bring him up, not just his mum.'

'So will they teach him how to use his trunk too?' Tom asked.

'They certainly will,' said Mrs Nightingale. 'They'll teach him all kinds of things. How to use his trunk to pull up grass. How to use his tusks to break off bark. How to pull a branch off a tree and use it as a fly swat.'

'Watching an elephant learn how to use his trunk is one of the most amazing things you'll ever see,' Mr Nightingale said, joining in. 'Shaurya will use it to breathe, smell, touch, say hello, grab things, throw things, fight, trumpet and suck up water. He'll even use it to breathe if he's underwater – like it's a snorkel. He'll be able to move it quickly and slowly, roughly and gently. He'll be able to use it to lift up a log or pick a flower.'

'Is it true that when they fight they deliberately tuck it out of the way, so it doesn't get hurt?' Sophie asked.

'Absolutely,' said Mrs Nightingale. 'An elephant without a trunk couldn't survive. It couldn't eat or drink for a start.'

'Couldn't it just bend down to pick up food?' Tom asked.

'They weigh about five tons,' said Mr Nightingale, 'and their legs are like columns. They have really short necks. They might be able to get their heads down on the ground, but they'd have serious problems trying to eat.'

'They also have thousands of air bubbles in their skulls,' Mrs Nightingale continued. 'To keep their heavy heads in the air. Without those air bubbles, their skulls would just go thump on the ground and they couldn't lift them.'

Tom and Sophie stared at the elephants crowding around Shaurya.

Sophie looked again at how the adults were using their trunks – stroking, curling, patting, snorting, squeezing and sniffing the air. Laila was curling her trunk around Frieda's.

Tom was imagining the air bubbles in Laila's head. He wondered if an elephant had ever got too many air bubbles in its head and started to take off like a helium balloon, its big legs flailing in the air. He was snapped out of his thoughts by a voice behind him.

'Isn't Shaurya handsome?'

It was Jane.

'He's a miracle,' said Sophie.

'Mum and Dad have been telling us all about elephants!' said Tom. 'How Shaurya's head is like a balloon.'

Jane chuckled. 'You know the best way of learning about elephants is to come and see the demonstration at midday.'

'Wow! Yeah!' said Tom. 'Will Shaurya be in it?'

'Not yet,' Jane smiled. 'He's a bit too young. Maybe next summer. But you'll see Frieda, Mist and Ricky.' She indicated the elephants in the field.

'I was in a show last week,' Tom said. 'I played the trumpet.'

But then he remembered how he'd played the wrong notes and he stopped talking.

Mrs Nightingale jumped in. 'We'll definitely come to the elephant show. But first things first. We haven't even had breakfast.'

During breakfast in the zoo cafe, Tom kept asking what the time was.

'It's OK, we've got ages,' said Mr Nightingale.

'Let's have a walk in the deer park first,' Mrs Nightingale suggested.

'It won't make us late for the elephants, will it?' Sophie asked, looking worried.

'Sophie, you know that's not till twelve,' Mrs Nightingale said with a smile.

Halfway through the deer park, Tom and Sophie asked – three times – whether it was twelve o'clock yet.

'OK, this is pointless,' said Mr Nightingale eventually. 'Let's just go to the arena now.'

'Cool!' said Tom.

'Great!' said Sophie.

It only took them a few minutes to walk there. The arena was just in front of the elephants' field, with seats arranged in banked semicircles.

'Now, the best view,' said Mrs Nightingale, 'is about four rows back. Just off to the side. That way, you can see everything.'

But Tom and Sophie had already sat down in the front row, right in the middle.

Mr and Mrs Nightingale looked at each other, shrugged and sat down next to their children.

They had fifty minutes to wait.

After about twenty minutes Tom asked, 'Why isn't it starting?'

'For goodness' sake, Tom, why do you think?' Mr Nightingale said.

After about thirty minutes Sophie said, 'This is taking for ever!'

'We could have gone round on the Jumbo Express. Twice,' Tom moaned.

Mr Nightingale sighed.

Ten minutes after this, another family arrived and sat just behind them.

'Told you we were a bit early,' said one of the grown-ups.

Over the next fifteen minutes, more people arrived and eventually the demonstration began.

Three elephants walked out into the arena. Frieda was first. Mist was next, holding Frieda's tail with her trunk, and Ricky was last, holding Mist's tail with his trunk. Jane and two of the other keepers followed them.

First, the elephants showed how they could fetch and carry. Ricky rolled a ball along the ground. Frieda picked up a log with her trunk. Mist pushed over a wooden column.

Jane was talking into a radio mike. 'Elephants clear paths through the jungle by pushing over trees and trampling down bushes,' she explained.

Next, Mist stood up on her hind legs and pointed her trunk straight up into the air, pulling down a branch that was suspended from a wooden beam.

'Everyone knows that giraffes are the tallest animal in the world,' Jane continued, 'but, if they use their trunk, elephants can reach even higher!'

After that, all three elephants balanced on small round podiums. Then they lay on their sides and lifted up their trunks.

'This is the safest way of washing an elephant's stomach,' Jane explained. 'Lying underneath an elephant is a seriously bad idea!'

At the end of the demonstration Tom and Sophie were quiet for a few minutes. Then they talked non-stop for over an hour.

Sophie said her favourite part was when the three elephants lay on their sides, but then changed her mind and said her it was when Mist stood up and reached the branch, and then Tom got annoyed because he said that was his favourite bit and that Sophie had just copied him.

Finally, when they were back in the zoo cafe eating their lunch, Tom asked his dad, 'Will Shaurya ever be in a show like that?'

Mr Nightingale nodded. 'Yes, he'll start his training when he's a few months old.'

'Cool!' Tom said. 'Can we help?'

'Unfortunately not,' said Mr Nightingale. 'An elephant has to be trained every day. And it takes months. And you're still at school.'

'Bloomin' school,' said Tom. 'Spoils every-thing.'

'Can we at least visit Shaurya every few weeks?' Sophie asked. 'To see how his training is going? To watch him prepare for the show?'

'What if I said no?' Mr Nightingale asked with a smile.

'Then I'd trample all over you!' said Sophie.

'And I'd drop a log on you,' said Tom.

'And then I'd pick you up with my trunk and hold you upside down over a mound of elephant poo,' Sophie declared.

'All right, you win . . .' Mr Nightingale said, holding up his hands. 'I'll say yes . . . !'

With that all agreed, Tom and Sophie tucked into lunch.

Chapter 6

The summer was whizzing by. Every morning Tom and Sophie would wake up, feed all the pets on the barge, eat breakfast and then climb into the van, ready to be driven to Whipsnade.

When they arrived at the zoo, they would rush to the elephants' field and spend at least half an hour talking to Jane about whether baby Shaurya had had enough sleep (five hours) and whether Laila had eaten enough breakfast (ten kilograms of hay and fifteen carrots).

Then their mother would arrive to check Shaurya's weight and height and general health and Tom and Sophie would demand an update.

After that, Tom would take pictures of Shaurya on his digital camera and Sophie would draw a picture of him in her sketchbook.

At twelve o'clock, they would go to the elephant demonstration. At one o'clock, they would meet their parents or their grandad or all three for lunch. After that, they tended to visit other animals before finally checking in on Shaurya again. Their father was usually there by then, leading the elephants out of the field and into the elephant house for the night.

In the evening on the barge, after their tea, they would clear everything off the dining-room table and open their Shaurya scrapbook. Tom would paste in any new photos and Sophie would add that day's sketch. If Shaurya had done anything new or different or memorable, Sophie would note it down.

Grandad would usually drop by just before bedtime, and he'd always ask to see the scrapbook.

'Is Shaurya taller than you yet, Tom?' he would ask.

It wasn't until the last day of the summer holidays that Tom was finally able to say, 'Yes.'

That evening, Tom and Sophie went to say goodbye to Shaurya. As a special treat, Jane let them into the elephant house and they were allowed to stroke Shaurya's back and feed his mother some carrots.

'When are you coming back then, kids?' Jane asked.

'We'll come and see him every three weeks,' said Sophie, holding out a carrot for Laila to grab with her trunk.

'And then we're going to stay for the WHOLE Christmas holidays,' said Tom.

'That's great timing!' said Jane. 'We'll probably start Shaurya's training then. You're going to love that!'

Tom asked Jane to take a photo of him and Sophie standing next to the young elephant. It was quite tricky because first Shaurya hid behind Laila, then he crept underneath her stomach, then he decided to have a drink of milk, before hiding behind Laila again.

In the end, the photo showed Tom and Sophie grinning next to Laila's bottom and a small grey smudge that looked a bit like Shaurya.

Back in London, the autumn term flew by. Tom and Sophie went to London Zoo every weekend, visiting their favourite animals and helping their parents however they could.

One Sunday, Tom spotted a penguin swallowing a coin that someone had thrown into the penguin pool and told the nearest keeper. Mrs Nightingale was able to give the penguin some medicine that stopped it getting zinc poisoning.

On a Saturday a few weeks later, Sophie helped her dad with a new arrival: an aardvark called Mabel. Mr Nightingale was responsible for designing its diet. Sophie did some research on the internet and found a range of pet food that closely resembled an aardvark's natural diet: ants, grubs and termites.

Every three weeks Grandad would drive Tom and Sophie to Whipsnade. They were always surprised by how big Shaurya was getting and how grown-up he was looking. They would scribble more notes and take more pictures and the Shaurya scrapbook got fatter and fatter.

Before they knew it, the Christmas holidays had come around. Tom and Sophie could barely contain their excitement as they sailed *The Ark* back up the Grand Union Canal towards Whipsnade Zoo, ready for two and a half weeks of uninterrupted Shaurya time.

'Do you think he'll have tusks yet?' Tom asked as they brushed their teeth on the first morning.

'Jane said not till he's two,' said Sophie, squeezing some toothpaste on to her brush.

'Imagine if *we* had tusks,' Tom said, taking the toothpaste from Sophie. 'It'd take us all day to brush them.'

'Yeah,' Sophic said, 'and a trip to the dentist would last flippin' hours.'

They both swilled, gargled and spat.

Jane was waiting for them at the elephants' field. She pointed at Shaurya and said, 'You're not going to believe what he's just started to do.'

Tom and Sophie watched as Shaurya trotted round and stood next to his mum.

Laila stretched out her trunk, picked up some of her breakfast hay and passed it into her mouth.

 As she started to chew, Shaurya put his trunk into his mother's mouth, pulled out some half chewed hay and transferred it into his own.

'He's started to eat solids!' Jane exclaimed.

'But . . . but why doesn't he just eat his own hay?' Tom asked.

'He's learning what food is safe to eat,' Jane said. 'If his mother's eating it, then he can eat it.'

'Oh no oh no oh no!' cried Sophie.

'What?' Jane said, spinning round.

'You've got to call Mum!' Sophie exclaimed. 'Laila just did a poo and Shaurya ate it.'

'It's OK, it's OK. Calm down,' said Jane. 'Elephant calves have to do that too. That lump of poo contains bacteria, and without that bacteria, Shaurya can't break down the grass he just ate. Elephants eat all kinds of weird things.'

'You're saying it gets weirder than poo?' asked Sophie.

'How about rocks?' Jane replied. 'In the wild, elephants have to eat rocks because of the salt they've got in them. They crunch them up like biscuits. In Africa, there are cave networks that only exist because of elephants munching their way through the rock.'

Tom took out his notebook. 'Shall I write down the eating rocks and poo thing? Or do you want to?'

Jane smiled as she watched them. 'This is all good news,' she went on. 'I told you we wanted to start training at Christmas. Well, now we can. Because Shaurya's eating hay, we can teach him some basic commands.'

Shaurya had ambled over towards Ricky and was asking to play, nudging Ricky with his head and trying to climb on his back.

'What's eating got to do with it?' Tom asked.

'Well, that's how we train him,' Jane explained. 'If he does something right, we give him some nice food. So he associates learning with getting a reward.'

'Blimey, I wish my school was like that,' said Tom. 'A bag of crisps every time I got a question right – I'd be top in everything!'

Jane chuckled. 'It does seem to work, I have to say. Anyway, we'll start Shaurya off tomorrow morning. I reckon by the end of your two weeks here, he'll be able to move forward and then stop. After that, it gets even more exciting.'

Tom and Sophie spent another half-hour talking to Jane and watching Shaurya and then they went off to  revisit the rest of the park. They watched the sea-lion demonstration and saw the giraffes being fed. About halfway through the afternoon Tom began to mumble something.

'What did you say?' Sophie asked.

'Back . . . soon . . . trumpet,' said Tom.

'I'm sorry, Tom, you'll have to speak up,' said Sophie.

'I said, I have to go back to the boat soon and practise my trumpet,' said Tom.

'Oh, OK,' said Sophie. 'I didn't realise . . .'

'There's a stupid Grade 3 exam that stupid Mrs Rogers wants me to do. And I stupidly said I'd do it,' said Tom.

'Good!' said Sophie. 'You should. You're great at playing the trumpet.'

'I'm not,' said Tom, 'but I'd better do it, because Freddy's doing it on oboe, and if you get to Grade 4, they put you in a special class where they let you play pop music and not just bloomin' classical.'

'OK,' said Sophie. 'I just want a quick look at the lemurs and then we'll go and find Grandad.'

The next morning Tom and Sophie arrived at the elephants' field three minutes after the zoo had opened. They had sprinted past the cloisters, run through the children's playground and scrambled over the railroad bridge. And now they were staring at the field, out of breath, their faces red and their chests heaving. But Shaurya and Laila were nowhere to be seen.

Their dad arrived a few minutes later, still working one of his arms into his zookeeper's uniform.

'Jane said they'd be training Shaurya this morning,' said Sophie.

'That's what she's doing,' said Mr Nightingale, doing up a button.

'So where is she? And where's Shaurya?' asked Tom.

'In the elephant house,' said Mr Nightingale. 'Shaurya needs to be somewhere calm and quiet. Where people can't see him.'

'So is Laila in there too?' Sophie asked.

'Of course,' said Mr Nightingale. 'Shaurya can't be separated from his mum. He'd freak out. She would too. Believe me, an elephant

freaking out is the last thing anyone wants! Come on.'

He led them to the elephant house and opened the door a fraction. Then he put a finger to his lips and pointed inside.

Tom and Sophie leaned forward and watched Shaurya's first morning of training. Jane was encouraging Shaurya to walk on command. Every time Shaurya took a step forward, Jane blew a whistle and gave Shaurya some food.

'He's good,' Mr Nightingale whispered, 'a really quick learner.'

They watched Shaurya's training for another ten minutes and then Mr Nightingale said they had better go, just in case they started to distract the elephants. They headed off to the cafe to get some breakfast.

'Dad,' Sophie said, as they approached the cafe.

'Yep,' said Mr Nightingale.

'What Jane is doing,' she said, 'the training, I mean. It's not . . . It's not cruel, is it?'

Mr Nightingale smiled and shook his head. 'I thought you might worry about that. But nothing we're doing is hurting or upsetting Shaurya. What's more, everything we train the elephants to do helps us to take care of them.'

He jerked his thumb over his shoulder.

'Think about it. At the moment, Shaurya is being trained to move forward and stop. If we didn't train him to follow us, how would we ever get him from one place to another? He weighs a ton already. Later we'll train him to lift up his legs. We need him to do this so we can file his

70

nails and inspect his feet for cuts. We'll train him to raise his trunk. That's so we can inspect his teeth and mouth. He'll also learn to lie on his side – so we can wash his chest and stomach. Otherwise we'd have to get underneath him and that's NOT a safe place for a zookeeper to be.'

'What about when he stands on his back legs?' asked Tom.

'That's something elephants do anyway,' said Mr Nightingale. 'We never get them to do anything unnatural. And besides, they're incredibly intelligent animals. They like to learn. They like tasks and challenges. It's part of our job to keep them stimulated.'

'I'm so going to be an elephant keeper when I grow up!' Tom said. 'I'll teach my elephants to stand on their heads!'

'Hmm,' said Mr Nightingale, 'that would probably kill them. Which I'm guessing would get you the sack.'

'OK,' said Tom, 'then I'll teach them to balance on their trunks!'

Mr Nightingale chuckled. 'Much more sensible,' he said.

They all went into the cafe and ordered some toast.

Chapter 7

Shaurya continued to be a brilliant student.

By the end of the Christmas holidays, he could follow Jane around the elephants' barn.

When Tom and Sophie came back for the February half-term, he could walk backwards and turn around on command.

By the Easter holidays, he could lie on his side, lie on his stomach and climb on to a podium.

By the end of the Easter holidays, he could lift up all four feet, one at a time, and pick up branches with his trunk.

By the time Tom and Sophie came back

for the May half-term, Jane had a surprise for them.

She asked Mr Nightingale to bring the children to the outdoor arena after the zoo was closed one Sunday. When they arrived, Jane was sitting in the middle of the front row. 'Welcome to the dress rehearsal,' she said with a smile.

'The dress rehearsal for what?' Sophie asked.

'Shaurya's first demonstration,' said Jane.

'You mean he's ready?' Tom and Sophie looked astonished.

'He can do everything now,' said Jane, 'and he's a natural show-off. See for yourselves.'

She disappeared behind a row of trees for a few minutes and then reappeared at the side of the arena. Laila, Shaurya and Frieda followed her into the arena, holding one another's tails with their trunks.

Tom and Sophie were spellbound. Shaurya still seemed so small next to Laila and Frieda, no more than a metre and a half tall, still covered with wiry fluff, not quite in control of his legs and trunk. But Jane was right – he clearly *loved* being part of the demonstration.

He rolled the ball across the arena with his trunk and then trumpeted loudly, looking very pleased with himself. Then he picked up a small log and carried it across to Jane. He balanced on a podium, lay down on his side, lay on his front, lifted up his feet and even picked up a flag with his trunk and waved it.

Mr Nightingale, Tom and Sophie were clapping and cheering.

At the end of the demonstration, Jane invited Tom and Sophie out on to the arena floor, where they patted Shaurya and gave him lots and lots of carrots.

'Tomorrow he'll meet the public,' said Jane.

'He's going to be a big star!' cried Tom.

'Well, he's already got a fan club, ' said Mr Nightingale, winking at Tom and Sophie.

The children chatted all the way home, their voices bubbling with excitement.

They barely slept that night – all they could think about was Shaurya's big debut. In the morning, they gave up on breakfast halfway through to start looking at their Shaurya scrapbook.

In the back of the van, on their way to Whipsnade, they talked non-stop about Shaurya's act and wondered which trick people would like the most.

Once they reached the zoo they helped their dad feed the zebras, but they barely gave the animals a glance – instead they talked about Shaurya's diet and eating habits.

Before they knew it, it was twelve o'clock, they were in the front row and the show was about to start.

The last nine months had led up to this moment. They had been there when Shaurya was born, they had watched him grow and learn, and now here he was, starring in his own demonstration! They felt a mixture of wonder and pride.

Tom had borrowed his dad's video camera. He was going to film everything.

Sophie had a camera and her sketchbook.

The show started.

For the first five minutes, everything went accordingly to plan. Shaurya rolled a ball across to Jane and then stood on his podium.

Then everything went wrong.

Shaurya, Frieda and Laila were about to lie down on their stomachs when Shaurya stumbled sideways. Had a noise given him a fright? Had something hit him? He started to back away, clearly distressed. Laila noticed immediately and moved to stand in front of him, flapping her ears

aggressively, rolling her huge head and trumpeting loudly.

People in the audience were starting to look confused and nervous. Jane was calming Laila down while another keeper fed Frieda some hay. The situation was quickly under control, but the audience were still looking restless.

'Is this all part of the demonstration?' called out one middle-aged woman.

'What's the matter with the baby one?' a young boy asked his parents loudly.

Tom and Sophie didn't know what to do. They could see that Laila had calmed down, but they understood why people were confused. Because they didn't know what was happening either.

Jane was now leading the elephants out of the arena. She was talking into her radio quietly.

Shaurya lolloped along behind his mother as if nothing had happened. Laila seemed unflustered too, flinging dust on her back with her trunk and whisking away flies with her tail.

One of the other keepers made an

announcement over the tannoy system: 'Sorry about the interruption, folks. One of our elephants is feeling under the weather. We'll restart the demonstration in an hour's time. See you then!'

People groaned and started to get to their feet.

'Well, this is most inconvenient!' huffed a woman with five children in tow.

'What shall we do?' Tom whispered to his sister. 'Shall we go too?'

'I don't know,' Sophie said.

'Shall we follow Jane and Shaurya?' Tom asked.

'No, Jane will have things to sort out,' said Sophie.

So they stayed where they were, sitting in the front row of the arena, staring at where Laila and Frieda and Shaurya had been just a few minutes before. The props for the demonstration – the balls and logs and branches and poles – were still lying on the ground.

Within a few minutes they were the only people

left sitting in the arena. Sophie looked down at the sketch she had made of Shaurya at the start of the demonstration. Tom realised that the video camera was still running and pressed 'Stop'.

It started to rain.

Chapter 8

That evening, Tom and Sophie were still reeling from the shock. What had happened to Shaurya? They just didn't get it.

They sat in the living room, with the TV on, not watching it, just staring blankly with their Shaurya scrapbook open between them.

'Snap out of it, you two,' Mr Nightingale said. 'It will be OK.'

'I checked out Laila and Shaurya,' said Mrs Nightingale, 'and they're both fine. No shock. No stress.'

But Tom and Sophie just grunted and nodded and continued to stare at nothing.

Eventually Sophie said, 'Jane said Shaurya won't be able to do another demonstration until they've worked out what went wrong.'

Tom added, 'She also said that they might wait a year before trying him out again. A year!'

Mr and Mrs Nightingale looked at each other and sighed.

'How about you come and help me feed the lions tomorrow?' Mr Nightingale suggested.

'Lions are rubbish,' said Tom. 'They don't do anything. They just lie around.'

'I'm giving the chimps their jabs in the morning,' said Mrs Nightingale. 'You could watch.'

'Chimps are silly,' said Sophie. 'They just swing on tyres. And throw fruit at each other.'

Mrs Nightingale shrugged. Mr Nightingale switched the TV over to the news. Tom and Sophie didn't even notice.

The children remained gloomy for a couple of days. They deliberately stayed away from the elephants. They didn't want to admit that they were annoyed with Shaurya or that they blamed him for what had happened. They wanted to remember him as the perfect elephant, the best elephant in the world, the elephant that could do anything.

Three days after the show, they bumped into Jane outside the cafe.

'How's Shaurya?' Tom and Sophie said at the same time.

'He's fine,' said Jane. 'We're getting no nearer

to working out what spooked him though. It's a mystery.'

'What have you been doing?' asked Sophie.

'Making loud noises to see if they make him jump,' said Jane. 'Scouring the arena for things he might have trodden on. You name it, we've tried it.'

Tom had an idea. 'You could watch the show again,' he said. 'That might make it easier to work out what upset him.'

'We would if we could, Tom,' said Jane. 'Only we weren't expecting any problems, you see, and none of us recorded it.'

'I did,' said Tom, 'on video. And Soph took pictures.'

'Really?' exclaimed Jane. 'What a stroke of luck! Blimey, you two are good!'

'We could look at the footage if you like,' said Tom.

'That would be great!' replied Jane.

'We'll solve the mystery in no time!' Sophie chipped in. 'You can count on us.'

Tom and Sophie raced off to the entrance gates, happy for the first time in days.

Jane watched them go and thought to herself, And I thought *I* was crazy about elephants!

Tom and Sophie went round to the staff changing rooms and found their father's locker. They knew the code off by heart. Tom took out the video camera and Sophie picked up her camera and her sketchbook. Then they went to the cafe and ordered two hot chocolates.

They started by poring over the video footage, watching it right through twice, and then in ten-second chunks. Sophie made notes in her sketchbook.

'This time,' she said, 'let's concentrate on the ground. See if there are any stones or bits of rubbish.'

Tom pressed 'Play' and 'Pause' and 'Play' again.

But it was no good. Neither of them could see anything that could have scared the little elephant.

'Let's try it one more time all the way through to see if we can spot anything we haven't thought of,' said Tom.

They were just at the section where Shaurya took his first step out into the arena when Sophie cried, 'There!'

'Where?' said Tom.

'There,' she said, 'a piece of glass.'

Tom zoomed in and they looked more closely. 'It's just a plastic wrapper,' he said glumly.

They rewound the video and watched it through again. This time, they turned the sound right up, listening for any noises.

About thirty seconds before Shaurya lost it, a keeper's van backfired just behind the arena, making a short, sharp bang like a firework.

'That could have been it,' said Tom.

'I don't know,' said Sophie. 'If it was just the van, then why didn't he panic straight away? Why wait half a minute?'

'They do do everything quite slowly,' Tom pointed out. 'Maybe they panic slowly too.'

'Maybe,' said Sophie doubtfully. They decided to note it down and tell Jane just in case. Then they watched the video one more time.

'Now let's look at everyone in the audience,' said Sophie. 'See if they did anything silly or unpredictable.'

'Good idea,' said Tom. He put his thumb down on 'Rewind'. 'I'll go back to the bit just before the elephants came in. Remember, when I did that 360-degree panorama and filmed everyone in the crowd.'

'I got some pictures of people watching too,' Sophie said, fiddling with her camera, and then she let out a loud gasp.

'There!' she said. 'Did you see it? That guy opened a can right next to Shaurya's ear!'

'Maybe it was that,' said Tom.

'And look at this photo,' said Sophie. 'Just at the same time this woman opened an umbrella. Maybe the sudden noise and the movement threw him.'

Tom found the woman on his video footage. 'But she's quite near the back. I think she'd be too far away for him to hear. The girl next to her though.'

'Oh yeah,' Sophie said. 'What's she doing with a party popper anyway?'

Tom was zooming in.

'She's wearing an "I am 6" badge. Probably her birthday,' he said.

'Hang on, look, she's just let it off,' said Sophie.

'Before Shaurya came into the arena,' added Tom, 'so it's probably not that.'

After another fifteen minutes of studying the film, they made a final list of what they'd found. As well as the van backfiring, the drinks can and the umbrella, they'd also spotted a small child exploding a crisp bag by accidentally sitting on it.

'Let's have one last look through the photos together,' said Sophie.

Behind the arena, Tom spotted an apple tree with lots of apples sitting around its roots.

'Do you think an apple could have hit him on the back?'

'We'd have noticed that,' said Sophie.

'But what if it hit the roof of that hut next to it? Maybe it made a loud bang. Or maybe two fell at the same time and made an even louder bang.'

'We'd have heard it on your video,' said Sophie.

'Maybe it was a hollow sound,' said Tom. 'You know, too deep for us to hear. Remember what Jane said about how elephants can hear sounds at low frequencies.'

Sophie nodded. 'Let's add it to the list.'

They read through their list again, put everything into Sophie's rucksack and headed for the elephants' field.

They all stood by the large barn where Shaurya slept. Jane was impressed. 'This is fantastic stuff, you two,' she said. 'We'll start working through these noises this afternoon.'

'What do you mean, you'll work through the noises?' Tom asked.

'Well, let's take the first thing here,' Jane explained. 'An umbrella opening. We'll find the noisiest umbrella in the zoo shop and open it when Shaurya least expects it. If he jumps or takes fright, then that's our culprit. Then we'll open it again and again, every morning. Till he's used to it. Till we know that it will never frighten him again.'

'Wow, can we come and watch?' asked Sophie.

'Only if you're very quiet,' said Jane, 'just in case it was YOU he was frightened of.'

Tom and Sophie smiled.

They met their parents and Grandad for lunch and told them what they'd discovered on the video and how Shaurya might have been startled by a loud noise.

'Good work, kids,' said Mr Nightingale. 'It sounds like you might be on to something. And with friends like you, Shaurya will be in a demonstration again in no time.'

'Do you mean to say you've got a whole film in that thing?' Grandad asked, pointing at the video camera. 'Why, it's the size of a pygmy shrew!'

After lunch, Tom and Sophie met Jane back at the elephant house. The children waited by the door while Jane went inside. They could see Laila and Shaurya standing inside on a layer of fresh straw while Jane and another keeper walked across to a bale of hay. On top of the hay, there was a banger, an umbrella, a crisp bag, a drink can, a cricket ball and a sheet of corrugated iron.

Tom and Sophie watched anxiously as Jane picked up the crisp bag, turned away from

Shaurya and blew air into it. Holding it behind her, she went up close to the elephant, whispering his name and stroking his bristly back.

Shaurya picked up some straw from the ground with his trunk and put it in his mouth.

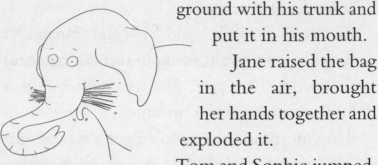

Jane raised the bag in the air, brought her hands together and exploded it.

Tom and Sophie jumped.

Shaurya calmly picked up another clump of straw, placed it on his tongue and slowly chewed. He hadn't reacted at all.

Then Jane tried the banger. This was meant to sound like a car backfiring.

Shaurya gave Jane a strange look and calmly chewed his straw.

He had the same reaction to the cricket ball bouncing on the iron sheet and the umbrella popping open.

'Just the drink can left to go,' said Sophie.

Jane shook the can and opened the ring pull, releasing a squirt of fizzy liquid.

This time, Shaurya and Laila turned round. Shaurya put his trunk out and sniffed the can. The finger at the end of his trunk started to grasp it.

'Oh no, you don't,' said Jane. 'This stuff rots your teeth.'

When Jane came out, she could tell that Tom and Sophie were disappointed.

'Don't worry,' said Jane. 'What you did really helped us.'

Tom said, 'No, it didn't. None of it scared Shaurya. We're back to square one.'

'But we've just crossed five things off our list,' said Jane. 'That's great progress.'

'I was CERTAIN it was going to be the drink can,' said Sophie.

'And I was SURE it was going to be the crisp bag,' said Tom.

'I thought it was going to be the car back-firing,' said Jane.

'But look, doesn't that mean that Shaurya's OK again? He's not scared of anything? He can do another demonstration. After all, we tried so many things,' said Tom.

Jane shook her head sadly. 'Sorry, Tom, but we couldn't risk it,' she said. 'We can't put any animal in a demonstration unless we know they're one hundred per cent happy with it. We don't want a repeat of what happened last time, do we? Until we've cracked this, Shaurya will have to wait in the wings.'

Tom and Sophie peered into the elephant house again and watched as Shaurya nuzzled his mother's side.

'Don't give up, kids,' said Jane.

'What else can we do?' Sophie asked.

'You'll think of something,' said Jane. 'I just know it.'

Chapter 9

Back on the barge that evening, Tom and Sophie were down in the dumps again. Their mum and dad had gone out to see a film, so Grandad was babysitting.

'Any luck with your baby elephant?' Grandad asked, as they tucked into takeaway pizza in front of the TV.

'No,' said Tom, 'we still can't work out what made him upset.'

'Well, elephants don't spook easily in my experience,' said Grandad. 'He must have seen something pretty scary. Or remembered something.'

'What do you mean "remembered"?' asked Sophie.

'Well, you know that elephants have incredible memories,' Grandad said.

'I know – an elephant never forgets,' said Tom.

'Well, it really doesn't,' said Grandad, wiping a bit of pizza off his chin. 'Memory is vital to an elephant. When I was out in Africa, there was a terrible drought. None of the elephants could find water. However, I saw one matriarch leading her herd towards a small group of hills. She looked very determined. I was intrigued so I followed them and, lo and behold, there was a small waterhole at the bottom of one of the slopes. Locals said that it had been fifty years since a pool had formed there. But this old elephant remembered. And saved her whole family.'

'Wow, that's amazing,' said Sophie.

'She was one of my favourite ever elephants,' said Grandad. 'Now, do you want any more spicy beef? No? No? All the more for me then. Anyway, another time, she stopped at a sand dune for about ten minutes. The rest of the herd stopped too. They were very quiet and seemed to be feeling the sand with their trunks. My local guide told me one of her brothers had died there thirty years before. The elephant recognised the spot. And stopped to think about him. It was just a patch of sand. No trees, no shrubs, no grass. But she remembered.'

'So hang on,' said Sophie. 'Maybe Shaurya was frightened by something he remembered.'

'Something that triggered a bad memory,' said Tom.

'But what?' Sophie wondered. 'We've got to look at that video again!'

'Hold on,' said Grandad. 'Before you go, can you show me how to change the television channel? I can't stand this American rubbish!'

But Tom and Sophie were already in their parents' bedroom, looking at the video footage on Mr Nightingale's computer.

'Go to the bit where Shaurya got upset,' Sophie said.

Tom clicked on fast forward and stopped at the part where Shaurya was backing away from the crowd. Tom and Sophie concentrated on what he was looking at.

'I can't work out what he's seen,' said Sophie.

'Neither can I,' said Tom.

'It's just a row of people,' said Sophie.

'Maybe it's that weird noise that's freaking him out,' said Tom.

'What weird noise?' said Sophie. 'I can't hear anything.'

'Not now, I mean when I was fast-forwarding,' said Tom.

He rewound and this time he turned the volume right up. Then he pressed 'Fast-Forward' and rewind and 'Fast-Forward'. The elephants were zipping backwards and forwards around the arena.

'Can you hear it now?' Tom asked.

Sophie nodded. As well as the sound of the

crowd – which had become a squeaking, chirp-
ing noise – a low, booming rumble was audible.
'And you know what?' she said.

Tom shook his head.

'I think that deep growling noise is coming
from Laila.'

'Really?' said Tom.

He watched the screen attentively.

'Blimey, you're right,' he said.

'Remember what Jane said,' Sophie said.
'Elephants communicate in these low noises that
we can barely hear. Remember how you can
record their voices and speed them up to hear
them. That's what we've done.'

'So Laila is telling Shaurya something,' said
Tom.

'I bet she's telling him to be careful,' said
Sophie.

Their grandad had appeared in the doorway.

'That's a noise I haven't heard in a long time,'
he said. 'An elephant's warning signal. One
elephant telling another to be on the lookout.'

'So it's not Shaurya remembering something,' said Tom. 'It's Laila!'

'We've been focusing on Shaurya all this time,' said Sophie, 'but really it was Laila that saw something she didn't like. SHE told Shaurya, and HE reacted.'

'So it's something Laila remembered,' said Tom. 'But what?' Sophie said.

They watched the video again, this time at normal speed. Now they were focusing on what Laila was looking at and where she was moving.

'This is where she starts to make that noise,' said Sophie.

'I must say, this is very clever,' said Grandad. 'You two must teach me all about computers.'

'Laila's not looking at anything in particular,' said Tom, 'except maybe that old tyre propped up against a tree.'

'I don't see why she'd be warning Shaurya about that,' said Sophie.

'She'll have her reasons,' said Grandad. 'Elephants understand cause and effect, you know.'

'What do you mean, "cause and effect"?' Tom asked.

'Well, they know that A leads to B which leads to C,' said Grandad. 'For example, in the wild, elephants often trample on lion cubs. Because they know they're going to grow into lions. And lions attack baby elephants.'

'That's pretty clever,' said Tom. 'Bit rough on the lion cub though.'

'Look, we're definitely going to need Jane's

help,' said Sophie. 'We have to pick her brains. It sounds as though Laila went through this whole thought process. She was thinking about something that MIGHT be dangerous. And that means we need to know what could have scared Laila in the past.'

'Well, Jane won't know much about Laila's past,' said Grandad. 'Jane can only be about twenty-five years old. And Laila's at least thirty.'

Tom and Sophie looked downhearted.

'You'll need to talk to someone who knew Laila as a calf,' said Grandad. 'Someone who was at the zoo twenty years ago. Someone who kept notes on all of the animals he looked after.'

'All the keepers look too young,' said Tom sadly.

'You pair of simpletons!' said Grandad. 'I'm talking about ME!'

Tom and Sophie both went, 'Ohhhhh!'

'I was Chief Vet, remember,' said Grandad. 'Come on, let's hop over on to my barge. See if we can't solve this mystery once and for all.'

The three of them leapt out of *The Ark* and trotted across the marina.

Half an hour later, they were in the living room of their grandad's barge, surrounded by folders, ring binders, scrapbooks, photographs, diaries and notebooks.

Grandad had one pair of glasses on – and another pair balanced on his forehead.

'No, not that folder,' he was saying. 'That's all about lions and tigers. Give me the blue one, Tom.'

Tom handed Grandad the blue folder.

'It says Regent's Park on it, Grandad,' said Tom, 'not Whipsnade.'

'Well, the elephants used to be in Regent's Park,' said Grandad, 'till people like me campaigned to change it. Elephants need space, and at Whipsnade they have space.'

He opened the folder.

'Bingo!' he said.

'Is it about the elephants?' Sophie asked.

'No, it's about Bingo,' said Grandad, 'one of my favourite sea otters. Let's try the yellow folder.'

Sophie took it down from the shelf.

As she opened it, a wedge of paper dropped out on to the floor. Photographs of elephants went everywhere.

'At last!' exclaimed Tom.

They soon found the section on Laila.

'Wow, is that her when she was born?' Sophie asked.

They were looking at a picture of a baby elephant.

'I think that's her brother,' said Grandad. 'He ended up going to the zoo in Berlin.'

'Why didn't he stay with Laila?' asked Tom.

'Because in the wild, boys get to a certain age, then leave the herd. Go off on their own. It would have been unnatural to keep him here.'

'So . . . so . . . Shaurya will be taken away?' Tom asked.

'Not till he's fourteen or fifteen,' Grandad said. 'You'll be in your twenties by then. You can follow him wherever he goes.'

He pointed at a sheaf of papers. 'This is what I was looking for,' said Grandad, 'my medical notes.' He pored through them.

'Bruised trunk at three months . . . cut her foot at six months . . . at eighteen months, head stuck in a tyre . . . at twenty months, got her head stuck again . . .'

'Hang on, Grandad, say that again,' Sophie said.

'Which bit?'

'The thing about the tyre.'

Grandad repeated the last part.

'That's it!' Sophie said.

Tom was nodding, his eyes wide.

'She was staring at a tyre,' Tom said.

'Making a warning sound,' said Sophie.

'Because she remembered how her head got stuck in one,' said Tom.

'I remember now,' said Grandad, his eyes getting misty. 'She was stuck for over an hour. Goodness knows how she got her head IN.'

'This is it, Tom, this is it,' Sophie said.

'We've got to tell Jane,' Tom said. 'I KNEW Shaurya wasn't scared of ANYTHING,' he added.

'Well, Jane won't be at Whipsnade now,' Grandad said. 'It's after nine. Time for one last slice of pizza and then bed.'

'Then we have to go FIRST THING in the morning,' said Tom.

'Yes, Jane said she was on the early shift tomorrow,' said Sophie. 'That means she'll be there at six. And so will we.'

'Six o'clock?' said Grandad. 'Ah, I don't know about that.'

'Come on. It'll be an adventure,' said Sophie.

Grandad's eyes lit up. 'I suppose it will. In fact, it definitely will. OK, you two. You're on. Meet you back here in exactly . . . hmm . . . eight hours, ten minutes and thirty-one seconds!'

Chapter 10

At 6.10 the following morning, Tom, Sophie and Grandad were in the elephant house. Jane was next to them, holding a spare tyre.

'So you're sure about this?' Jane asked.

Tom, Sophie and Grandad all nodded.

'A tyre,' said Jane. 'A rubber tyre?'

Tom, Sophie and Grandad nodded again.

Jane walked into the elephant house holding the tyre. Tom, Sophie and Grandad followed her.

Jane crunched across the straw to where Shaurya and Laila were standing.

As soon as she got within ten metres of the two elephants, Laila snorted and spread her ears

to make her head as big and threatening as possible.

'It's just a tyre, darling,' Jane said. 'Just a harmless tyre.'

But Laila was standing between the tyre and Shaurya, stamping her feet and flapping her ears.

Jane backed away, looking over her shoulder at Grandad with an astonished look on her face.

'Who'd have thought it?' she said.

'So now you know what caused it,' Tom said, 'Shaurya can appear in the next demonstration.'

'I wish it was that simple,' Jane said. 'We can't let Shaurya out without his mother, and we can't let Laila out till we've convinced HER that tyres aren't scary.'

'But can't you just make sure there are no tyres in the arena?' Sophie asked.

'We can't take the risk,' said Jane. 'After all, the tyre she saw wasn't meant to be there. Obviously, it was left there by one of the keepers – maybe they'd been cleaning out the chimp enclosure and left it there, intending to pick it up later. Wouldn't have known about Laila's phobia.'

'But we have to go back to school next week,' Tom said. 'We really want to see Shaurya in a demonstration again.'

'Sorry,' said Jane, 'but we're going to have to show Laila a tyre every morning for weeks – big tyres, small tyres, pink tyres, blue tyres – till she doesn't see them as a threat.'

'Are you SURE Shaurya can't go onstage without his mother?' Tom asked. 'He is very brave.'

Jane shook her head.

'But listen,' she said, 'what you did was amazing. Amazing. Laila would thank you if she could. You took the time to work out what she was saying. To find out what was distressing her. To study her childhood. We're not technically allowed to do this, but I think you should join us for our morning walk.'

'What do you mean?' Tom asked.

'Well, it's dawn,' said Jane, 'we often take the elephants out to see the sunrise. Have you ever ridden an elephant across a field before?'

Tom and Sophie looked at each other.

'Er . . . ah . . . I haven't,' said Sophie. 'How about you, Tom?'

'Er . . . ah . . . no,' said Tom.

'Watch me then,' said Jane. She gave the command for Laila to left her right foot. Jane put her own foot on Laila's knee. Then she grabbed the tough roll of flesh at the top of Laila's ear. As Laila lifted her leg up even higher, Jane was swung round on to the elephant's back.

'See? Simple,' Jane said. She slid down and said, 'Now it's your turn.'

So that morning the elephants were led out across the hills behind Whipsnade.

They grazed on the low trees and roamed through the long grass.

They drank water from streams and squelched across muddy ditches.

The elephants stood watching the sunrise, curling their trunks around each other and making low, contented rumbling sounds.

On Laila's back, you could see two children silhouetted against the morning sun.

After a few minutes, the children gave the 'Forward' command, and Laila moved off, rocking her passengers back and forth as she strode through the fields and led the herd back home.

Chapter 11

Three weeks later, and Shaurya was back in the arena.

It was term time for Tom and Sophie and they were back at school in London. But they came up to Whipsnade specially to watch Shaurya. And he didn't put a foot wrong. The audience loved him.

Two weeks after that, Tom's music teacher, Mrs Purcell, asked Tom if he would play a solo in this summer concert. Tom, without thinking, said yes.

At home that night, panic set in.

'I can't do it, I can't do it,' he said to Sophie.

'What are you talking about?' asked Sophie. 'You're even better than you were last year. And last year, you were great.'

'No, I wasn't,' said Tom. 'Don't you remember? I played all the wrong notes.'

'I know that's what you heard,' said Sophie, 'but it's not what *we* heard. Maybe you can hear really low frequencies – like Laila.'

Tom smiled.

'Besides, you've got to get over it,' said Sophie. 'You can't let one case of stage fright ruin your life. Look at Laila and Shaurya.'

'What do you mean?' Tom asked.

'Practise the piece every day,' said Sophie. 'Play it in front of Freddy. Play it in front of us. Play it in front of your class. Till you're sick of it.'

Tom groaned. 'Sounds too much like hard work to me.'

'OK, well you'd better tell Mrs Purcell you don't want to do it then,' said Sophie. 'Tell her you're scared of other people, you're rubbish at the trumpet and you want to play the triangle instead.'

'No way!' Tom said.

He had left his trumpet on the armchair. Sophie picked it up.

'Then play me the piece,' she said, handing the trumpet to her brother.

She sat on the armchair and folded her arms.

Tom looked at the trumpet.

'Come on,' Sophie said, 'scaredy-cat.'

Tom frowned and started to play.

He got to the end without fluffing any notes and looked up at Sophie.

'That was beautiful,' Sophie said. 'Play it again.'

'Nooo,' Tom howled.

'Chicken,' said Sophie. 'Coward.'

Tom sighed and started again from the beginning.

For the next few days, Tom practised and practised. He played for his parents and his grandad.

He staged a small concert in the marina where he stood on top of the barge and played to the other houseboat owners. He played outside the supermarket on Camden High Street and earned £3.17 from passers-by.

On the night of the concert, he was still nervous.

He was standing backstage with Freddy.

'I'm going to do what I did last year,' said Freddy, 'and just pretend to play.'

'But Mrs Purcell rumbled you,' said Tom.

'She won't this year,' Freddy said.

He pointed to a small speaker that he had taped inside the end of his oboe. Then he lifted an MP3 player out of his pocket. He pressed Play and his oboe appeared to be playing itself.

'Neat, eh,' Freddy said.

'But that's not the song we're playing,' said Tom.

'What are you talking about?' Freddy said.

'That's "Jerusalem",' said Tom. 'We're play-ing "Food, Glorious Food".'

'Oh man!' Freddy said, prodding frantically at his MP3 player, 'I haven't got that on here. Who's it by?'

'I dunno,' said Tom. 'Oliver Twist, I think.'

'OK, everyone,' Mrs Purcell announced, 'one minute to go.'

'You'll be fine, Freddy,' said Tom, 'you've played it fifty times. And anyway, if you play a few wrong notes, it doesn't matter, does it? It's only mums and dads out there. Just think of it as a great opportunity for showing off.'

Freddy nodded and looked sadly at his oboe. A wire was hanging out of the end. 'It took me hours to set this up,' he said.

And then it was time to go on.

Tom and Freddy were both excellent. Freddy decided to twirl his oboe around and play it as loud as he could, as if he was a rock star with an electric guitar. Mrs Purcell frowned but the audience laughed.

Then it was Tom's solo.

He played the first two notes perfectly. The third note was a bit wobbly.

Everything seemed to slow down as he thought about playing the fourth.

Sophie was in the audience. She could see Tom's face dropping.

'Come on, Tom,' she whispered. 'Just ride it out.'

Tom shook off his fear and launched himself into the rest of his solo. It was the best he'd ever played it.

The audience burst into rapturous applause.

The rest of the orchestra came back in and finished the piece.

Then everyone got a standing ovation.

As they walked offstage, Freddy slapped Tom's back.

'You were good, Tombo,' he said, 'but I was the best.'

There was a voice behind them.

'Frederick Finch,' Mrs Purcell said, 'I'd like a word with you.'

'Man!' Freddy protested. 'What did I do THIS time?'

Tom put his trumpet back in its case and said goodbye to the rest of his friends before going over to greet his parents.

Mr and Mrs Nightingale gave him a huge hug. Grandad barked, 'Bravo!'

They walked out of the hall together.

Sophie said quietly, 'Well done, Tom. Shaurya would be proud of you.'

'To be honest,' said Tom, 'I pretended to BE Shaurya. I imagined the trumpet was my trunk!'

Sophie smiled.

'I became half-elephant,' said Tom.

'Only half?'

'OK, three-quarters,' said Tom. He held his trumpet to his lips and blew as hard as he could.

His parents twisted round in surprise.

'Sorry,' Tom said. 'That's what we elephants do when we're excited.'

Mr and Mrs Nightingale looked at each other, smiled and shook their heads.

'Come on then, Shaurya,' said Mr Nightingale. 'It's time to hit the hay!'

Zoological Society of London

ZSL London Zoo is a very famous part of the
Zoological Society of London (ZSL).

For almost two hundred years, we have been
working tirelessly to provide hope and a
home to thousands of animals.

And it's not just the animals at ZSL's Zoos in
London and Whipsnade that we are caring for.
Our conservationists are working in more than
50 countries to help protect animals in the wild.

But all of this wouldn't be possible without your help.
As a charity we rely entirely on the generosity of our
supporters to continue this vital work.

By buying this book, you have made an essential
contribution to help protect animals.
Thank you.

Find out more at **zsl.org**